THE
ITSY BITSY
SPIDER

THE
ITSY BITSY
SPIDER

As told and illustrated by
Iza Trapani

Scholastic Inc.
New York   Toronto   London   Auckland   Sydney

A huge thanks to Kim and Dan Adlerman for their input and enthusiasm in producing this book

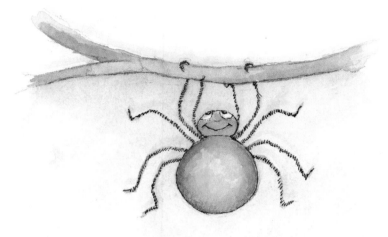

ISBN 0-590-69821-4

30 29 28 27 26 25 24   1/0

Printed in the U.S.A.   08

First Scholastic printing, January 1996

FOR MY NIECES—BEATA,
EMILIA, AND ROSIE, WITH LOVE

The itsy bitsy spider
Climbed up the waterspout.

Down came the rain
And washed the spider out.

Out came the sun
And dried up all the rain,
And the itsy bitsy spider
Climbed up the spout again.

The itsy bitsy spider
Climbed up the kitchen wall.

Swoosh! went the fan
And made the spider fall.

Off went the fan.
No longer did it blow.
So the itsy bitsy spider
Back up the wall did go.

The itsy bitsy spider
Climbed up the yellow pail.

In came a mouse
And flicked her with his tail.

Down fell the spider.
The mouse ran out the door.
Then the itsy bitsy spider
Climbed up the pail once more.

The itsy bitsy spider
Climbed up the rocking chair.

Up jumped a cat
And knocked her in the air.

Down plopped the cat
And when he was asleep,
The itsy bitsy spider
Back up the chair did creep.

The itsy bitsy spider
Climbed up the maple tree.

She slipped on some dew
And landed next to me.

Out came the sun
And when the tree was dry,
The itsy bitsy spider
Gave it one more try.

The itsy bitsy spider
Climbed up without a stop.

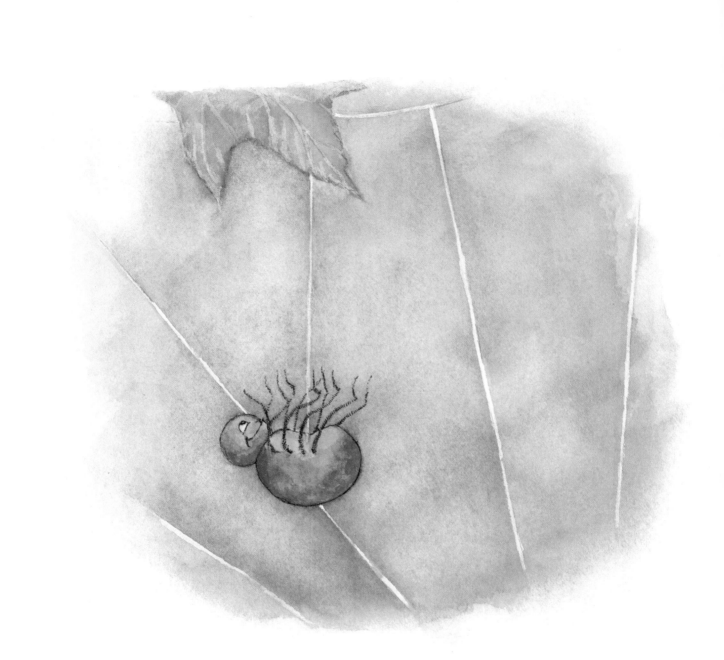

She spun a silky web
Right at the very top.

She wove and she spun
And when her web was done,